WE WERE PERFECT UNTIL WE WEREN'T

A TALE OF ALMOSTS AND GOODBYES

AGAMPREET SINGH

Contents

Preface

Love, in its purest and most raw form, often finds its first expression in our teenage years. It's during these formative moments that our hearts learn to beat for another, our minds begin to understand the complexities of human connection, and our souls experience the exquisite pleasure and pain of romantic attachment. **"WE WERE PERFECT UNTIL WE WEREN'T"** invites readers into this delicate world of first love, where every glance holds promise and every heartbeat carries the weight of endless possibilities. In the corridors of adolescence, where emotions run deep and feelings burn bright, we meet Prateek and Meher, two young souls whose lives intertwine in the most ordinary of settings – a school van. Their story, while unique in its details, mirrors the universal experience of teenage love that has shaped countless lives across generations. Through their journey, we explore the profound impact of first love and its lasting imprint on our emotional landscape. This book delves deep into the intricate dance of teenage romance, setting itself apart from typical young adult narratives by presenting an unflinchingly honest portrayal of both the euphoric highs and devastating lows of first love. Unlike many contemporary works that either romanticize or trivialize teenage relationships, this story acknowledges the genuine depth of young love while respecting its inherent vulnerability and transient nature. The narrative weaves together several compelling themes that resonate with both young readers and those who remember their own first loves. At its core, the book explores the nature of emotional attachment and the profound impact of first romantic connections. It examines how these early experiences shape our understanding of love, trust, and personal identity. The theme of growth and transformation runs throughout the story, as both Prateek and Meher navigate the complex waters of their evolving relationship and individual development. The book also tackles the difficult subject of loss and resilience, showing how young hearts learn to cope with disappointment and change. The raw authenticity of teenage emotions is captured in vivid detail, from the electric excitement of first attraction to the crushing weight of heartbreak. Through Prateek's perspective, readers experience the intoxicating rush of new love, the confusion of changing dynamics, and the gut wrenching pain of watching someone slip away. The story doesn't shy away from exploring the intense emotions that characterize teenage relationships, validating these feelings while providing insight into their nature and impact. While primarily written for young adults navigating their own romantic journeys, this book speaks to anyone who has ever experienced the transformative power of first love. Parents will find valuable insights into the emotional world of their teenagers, while older readers might recognize echoes of their own past experiences. The story serves as both a mirror for current experiences and a window into the universal nature of young love. The narrative follows the evolution of Prateek and Meher's relationship with careful attention to the subtle shifts in dynamics that often precede major changes. From their first meeting in the school van to their eventual separation, each moment is treated with the gravity it deserves in the context of teenage experience. The book explores how external factors such as peer pressure, social dynamics, and personal growth influence young relationships, providing readers with a comprehensive understanding of the forces that shape teenage romance.Through Prateek's journey, readers will gain insight into the complexity of emotional attachment and the importance of self-discovery during adolescence.

CHAPTER ONE

THE FIRST GLANCE

The morning sun cast long shadows across the crowded school parking lot as students shuffled their way toward the aging fleet of yellow vans. Among them walked Prateek, a lanky fifteen-year-old who perpetually seemed to mirror his general state of mind. His worn backpack hung loosely from one shoulder, weighted down with textbooks and the countless thoughts that occupied his teenage mind. The familiar screech of rubber against asphalt marked the arrival of Van , its weathered exterior bearing testament to years of faithful service transporting students to and from Sir Padampat Singhania Education Centre. Prateek had grown accustomed to this daily ritual, climbing into the van with practiced ease, finding his usual spot near the window, where the suspension wasn't quite as jarring and the morning conversations of his fellow students provided a comfortable background noise to his thoughts.

That particular May morning, however, proved to be anything but ordinary. As Prateek settled into his seat, absently gazing out the window at the gathering crowd of students, a flash of movement caught his attention. A girl he had never seen before was making her way toward the van, her presence immediately commanding attention without any apparent effort on her part. Her name, as he would soon learn, was Meher Kaur.

Meher possessed the kind of natural grace that made even the simple act of climbing into a school van seem somehow elegant. Her long black hair was pulled back swinging gently as she moved, and her warm black eyes seemed to hold a constant glimmer of amusement, as if she was a fairy or any angel. She wore the standard school uniform – a white shirt and navy blue skirt – but somehow managed to make it look less like a uniform and more like a conscious fashion choice. The van's interior suddenly felt smaller, more intimate, as Meher made her way down the narrow aisle. With the only available seat being the one next to Prateek, she paused briefly before sitting down. "Is this seat taken?" she asked, her voice carrying a musical quality that immediately fetched itself into Prateek's memory. He managed to shake his head, trying to appear casual while his heart performed an unexpected gymnastics in his chest. As the van moved forward, beginning its journey through the buzzing streets of Kanpur, Prateek found himself attentive of every movement, every breath, every slight shift in position that brought him into the boundary of Meher's presence. The familiar route to school suddenly seemed new and exciting, each turn and bump in the road an opportunity for their shoulders to brush accidentally, each stop a chance to steal a glance at his new seat companion. Meher, as it turned out, she had changed her school, having moved to SPSEC over the summer. This information came out naturally during the course of their first conversation, which began when Meher talked to fellow students sitting beside her. That simple literary reference opened the floodgates of conversation. Prateek, usually reserved and thoughtful, found himself engaging in an animated discussion about books, music, shoes and the universal experience of being the new kid – though in Meher's case, she with an desirable confidence that Prateek couldn't help but admire. Their conversation flowed effortlessly, punctuated by the steady rhythm of the van's movement and the background chatter of other students. Prateek learned that Meher was an only child in her family; and that she had a passion for dance that had already earned her recognition in several competitions. She spoke about her former school SIPS with a hint of nostalgia but also with an excitement about the new chapter beginning in SPSEC.

As they talked, Prateek found himself increasingly drawn to the way Meher's eyes crinkled at the corners when she smiled, how she used her hands expressively when describing something she was passionate about, and the genuine interest she showed when he spoke about his own life. He told her about his dreams, his love for cars, his interest in other activities. The usual fifteen minute journey seemed to pass in mere minutes, and when the van finally pulled up to the school gates, Prateek felt a surprising ache of disappointment. As they gathered their belongings and prepared to leave, Meher turned to him with that same warm smile that had first caught his attention. "Thanks for making my first day a little less scary," she said, and in that moment, Prateek felt something shift inside him, like the first note of a song he hadn't known he'd been waiting to hear. Watching her walk away toward the school building, Prateek realized that his world had tilted slightly on its axis.

The morning sun caught the edges of her hair, creating a momentary halo effect that seemed to perfectly summarize the magic of their first encounter. He stood there, rooted to the spot, until his best friend's voice cut through his vision, teasing him about his obvious staring. That evening, as Prateek lay in bed replaying every moment of their conversation, analyzing every smile and casual touch, he couldn't help but feel that something significant had begun. The memory of Meher's laugh, the way she listened so intently when he spoke, and the natural ease of their interaction had planted a seed of hope in his heart. Little did he know that this was just the beginning of a journey that would reshape his understanding of love, friendship, and the complex landscape of teenage emotions. Tomorrow couldn't come soon enough, and for the first time in his life, Prateek found himself looking forward to the school van ride with an anticipation that made his heart race. The daily routine that had once seemed so dull now held the promise of something extraordinary, all because of a chance seating arrangement and a girl named Meher who had unknowingly stepped into his world and changed its color palette entirely.

CHAPTER TWO

GROWING AFFECTION

The early morning sunlight filtered through the van's windows, casting a warm glow on the faces of drowsy students making their way to school. In the weeks following their first encounter, Prateek found himself increasingly drawn to the rhythmic pattern of Meher's presence in his daily commute. The school van, once merely a means of transportation, had transformed into a sanctuary of shared moments and subtle exchanges that made his heart flutter with anticipation each morning. Meher's habitual unpunctuality became a source of endearing amusement for Prateek. He would watch from his window seat as she hurriedly approached the van, her dark hair catching the morning light, sometimes still adjusting her backpack. These small, unguarded moments painted a picture of authenticity that captivated him more than any carefully curated social media profile ever could.

Their conversations began hesitantly, like most teenage interactions do. Weather observations evolved into discussions about shared talks, which gradually deepened into exchanges about their favorite music and movies. Prateek discovered that Meher had a wide taste in music, ranging from Punjabi to English songs. He found himself downloading songs she mentioned in passing, secretly creating a playlist that would remind him of their conversations. The backseat of the van became their unofficial territory, where they would share earbuds and listen to music together during the longer stretches of traffic. Prateek remembered vividly the first time their hands accidentally brushed while reaching for a fallen earbud. The electric current that seemed to pass between them in that brief moment left him speechless for several minutes, while Meher continued chatting, seemingly unaffected, about her upcoming mathematics test. Their friendship blossomed in these narrow quarters, punctuated by the stop-and-go rhythm of city traffic. Meher's playful nature emerged gradually, like sunshine breaking through morning clouds. She would often tease Prateek about his past crushes whenever he shared insights about his past experiences with other people. Her laughter, bright and uninhibited, became the soundtrack to their morning journeys.

As weeks passed, Prateek found himself arriving earlier at his pickup point, eager to secure their preferred seating arrangement. He noticed how Meher would sometimes save him a spot, placing her bag on the seat next to her and removing it with a smile when he boarded. These small gestures spoke volumes in the language of teenage affection, where direct words often failed to capture the complexity of emerging feelings. Other students in the van began to notice their growing closeness. Knowing looks were exchanged, and occasional whispers circulated, but Prateek barely registered them. His world had narrowed to these precious minutes spent in Meher's company, where every shared joke and casual touch added another layer to his growing affection. He found himself looking forward to Mondays, a sentiment that puzzled his weekend-loving friends who didn't share his daily commute with someone special. Meher's responses to his attention were precise yet encouraging. She would often seek his opinion on matters ranging from school projects to family decisions, valuing his perspective in a way that made him feel both important and nervous. When she would lean closer to show him something on her phone, the scent of her shampoo would briefly override his ability to focus on whatever she was trying to share. Their conversations began to extend beyond the confines of the van through text messages and social media interactions.

Prateek would spend hours crafting the perfect response to her casual messages, analyzing every word choice and emoji placement. He saved screenshots of their conversations, returning to them late at night when the house was quiet and his thoughts were free to wander through the landscape of possibilities their friendship presented.

As their connection deepened, Prateek noticed changes in himself. He began paying more attention to his appearance, making sure his uniform was properly pressed and his hair neatly styled before leaving home. He developed a sudden interest in the movies she mentioned watching, even though romantic, fictional movies had never been his preferred genre. His friends noticed these changes, teasing him good naturedly about his "van crush," but he couldn't bring himself to care about their playful punches. The van became a symbol of their developing relationship, where every shared glance and whispered conversation added another thread to the curtain of their connection.

Even on days when conversation was minimal, comfortable silence would settle between them like a warm blanket, punctuated only by the soft sound of shared music through split earbuds. As they approached the end of the term, Prateek's feelings had grown from a spark of interest into something more profound. He found himself wondering about her during classes, his mind drifting to their morning conversations when he should have been focusing on lectures. The way she would absently twirl a strand of hair while talking, or how her eyes would crinkle at the corners when she smiled genuinely, became details he treasured and replayed in his mind.

CHAPTER THREE

A SPARK IGNITES

The gentle hum of the school van's engine had become a familiar soundtrack to Prateek's daily routine, but today felt different. After weeks of sharing meaningful glances and stolen moments of conversation with Meher, the weight of his unspoken feelings had become unbearable.

The morning sun filtered through the van's windows, casting a soft glow on Meher's face as she sat in her usual spot. That morning, Prateek had woken up with a resolve that surprised even himself. The previous night had been spent tossing and turning, his mind replaying every interaction they'd shared, every laugh that had echoed through the van's confined space, and every moment their eyes had met in silent understanding. He had written and rewritten his confession countless times in his head, each version more elaborate than the last, but none seemed adequate to express the depth of what he felt. As they neared their usual drop-off point, all the students left the van. Prateek was waiting for Meher to come out so that he could tell her what he felt, but after looking at her beauty, he forgot all his words. The world seemed to slow down as they stepped away from the van. Prateek's courage also left him, and his hands trembled slightly as he struggled to find the right words—but he couldn't find them.

So the day passed as usual, and both of them returned to their homes. At the end of the day, both were having social media talks. At that moment, Prateek decided to express his feelings to her.

Then he wrote a paragraph with his hands shaking, and his heartbeats reached their maximum heights. The seconds that followed felt like an eternity as Meher processed his words.

Their first proper conversation outside of school happened when Prateek suggested they meet in a cafe. They sat together, their shoulders occasionally brushing against each other. Meher spoke about her dreams, her eyes lighting up as she described the stories she wanted to tell. Prateek listened intently, mesmerized by this new side of her he was discovering. "I never told anyone about my dreams before," Meher admitted. "It feels different with you, like I can be myself without worrying about being judged." Prateek's heart swelled at her words, and in that moment, she gathered the courage to reach for his hand. He didn't pull away, instead intertwining his fingers with hers in a gesture that felt both natural and extraordinary. Their conversation flowed effortlessly, touching on everything from their dreams and some random talks to their family lives. Prateek got to know that she wanted to learn how to play guitar, but she didn't know that Prateek had already joined guitar classes. He told her about his passion for learning guitar. After having some random talks, it was time to say goodbye. Prateek didn't want her to go, so he gave her a kiss on her cheek. With Meher's blush, they left the place.

CHAPTER FOUR

THE HIGHS OF YOUNG LOVE

Having finally confessed their feelings for each other, Prateek and Meher's relationship blossomed into something beautiful and tender, characteristic of first love's pure intensity. The school van, once just a mode of transportation, had transformed into their sanctuary, where every shared glance held meaning and each accidental touch sent electricity through their young hearts. Prateek found himself counting minutes until he could see Meher again, their morning van rides becoming the highlight of his day. He noticed how she would always save him a seat, her backpack purposively placed to reserve his spot beside her. The way she would lean slightly towards him when laughing at his jokes, her shoulder brushing against his, created butterflies in his stomach that refused to settle. These simple moments, seemingly insignificant to others, painted his world in vibrant colors he had never experienced before.

During school events, their connection became even more apparent. At the Inter-House Dance Competition, watching Meher dance, her determination and grace as she started— hair streaming behind her like a banner of golden sunshine— made his heart swell with pride and affection. When her house had won second place, her eyes immediately sought his in the crowd, and their shared smile held more meaning than any medal could convey. It was in these moments that Prateek realized how deeply he had fallen for her. Their friend circle expanded naturally, as couples often attract other couples and friendly observers. During lunch breaks, they would sit with their growing group of friends but somehow manage to create their own private world within the chaos of the cafeteria. Their friends would tease them about being "that couple," but Prateek secretly reveled in these comments, proud to be associated with someone as special as Meher. Their text messages would often continue late into the night, discussing everything from their dreams for the future to their favorite ice cream flavors. Prateek found himself opening up about things he'd never shared with anyone else—his fears about not living up to his parents' expectations, his secret desire to become a writer, his childhood memories that shaped who he was. Meher listened with genuine interest, offering perspectives that often surprised him with their depth and understanding. Their relationship wasn't without its playful moments either. Meher had a talent for making even the most ordinary situations extraordinary.

As their relationship deepened, Prateek found himself noticing and treasuring the smallest details about Meher—the way she would rub her nose when concentrating on a difficult math problem, how she always tied her hair in a messy bun during physics practical classes, the particular tone her laugh took when she was truly amused versus when she was being polite. Each discovery felt like finding a new treasure, making him fall even deeper in love with her. Their friends often commented on how well they complemented each other. Where Prateek was quiet and thoughtful, Meher was outgoing and spontaneous. She brought out a side of him that he didn't know existed— someone who could be silly, who could take risks, who could love without reservation. In return, he provided a steady presence in her life, someone who would listen without judgment and support her dreams unconditionally. The van rides till home became their time to decompress and share their days with each other. Even when they had spent most of the day together, there was always something new to discuss, some detail to share, some feeling to express. The other students in the van had grown used to their quiet conversations and shared earbuds as they listened to songs that would become the soundtrack of their love story.

Looking back, Prateek would later realize that these were the golden days of their relationship. Every moment felt charged with possibility, every interaction filled with the pure joy of young love. Even their disagreements were minor and quickly resolved, usually ending with shared laughter and a stronger understanding. The world seemed to spin differently when they were together, as if their love had created its own gravity, pulling them into an orbit that felt both exciting and safe. Yet, as perfect as things seemed, there were moments when Prateek caught glimpses of something in Meher's eyes—a fleeting shadow, a brief hesitation—that he couldn't quite understand. But in the bliss of young love, these moments were easy to dismiss, lost in the overwhelming happiness of their connection. After all, what could possibly go wrong when everything felt so right?

CHAPTER FIVE

CRACKS IN THE FANTASY

As we transition from the blissful highs of young love explored in the previous chapter, we now enter a phase where the rosy tint of romance begins to fade, revealing the complexities and challenges that often accompany teenage relationships.

The once-perfect picture of Prateek and Meher's love story starts to show signs of wear, as subtle yet significant changes emerge in their dynamic. Meher's behavior undergoes a gradual but noticeable shift. The girl who once eagerly awaited Prateek's presence in the school van now seems distracted, her enthusiasm dimmed. Where she once leaned into conversations with excitement, she now appears withdrawn, her responses becoming shorter and less engaging. Prateek, ever attuned to Meher's moods, can't help but notice these changes, though he initially tries to dismiss them as temporary mood swings. At first, the changes were so slight that Prateek questions whether he's imagining things. Perhaps Meher is just tired from her increased involvement in extracurricular activities, he reasons. Or maybe she's stressed about upcoming exams. He recalls a conversation they had just a week ago, where Meher mentioned feeling overwhelmed by her academic workload. "I just need to focus more on my studies," she had said, her eyes not quite meeting his. At the time, Prateek had nodded understandingly, offering his support. Now, he wonders if there was more to that statement than he initially realized.

As days pass, the changes become harder to ignore. Meher's text messages, once filled with heart emojis and playful banter, become increasingly infrequent and brief. Their daily conversations in the school van, which used to flow effortlessly for the entire journey, now often lapse into uncomfortable silences. Prateek finds himself struggling to find topics that engage Meher's interest, his attempts at humor met with polite smiles rather than the genuine laughter he's grown accustomed to. Confusion clouds Prateek's thoughts as he grapples with this new reality. He replays recent interactions in his mind, searching for any misstep on his part that might have caused this shift. Did he say something wrong? Was he not attentive enough? The questions swirl in his mind, leaving him feeling increasingly insecure and anxious about the state of their relationship. In an attempt to understand and possibly remedy the situation, Prateek tries to initiate more one-on-one time with Meher outside of school. He suggests studying together on video calls, hoping that a change of scenery might reignite their connection. Meher agrees, but her appearance during these calls is markedly different from before. She seems distracted, her eyes often wandering to her phone or out the window, as if searching for an escape. Prateek's attempts at deep conversation are met with noncommittal responses, leaving him feeling more disconnected than ever.

As Prateek struggles to make sense of these changes, he begins to notice external factors that may be influencing their relationship. The social dynamics of high school are complex and ever-changing, and Prateek realizes that he and Meher are not immune to these pressures. He observes Meher spending more time with a new group of friends, girls known for their popularity and active social lives. While Prateek has always supported Meher's friendships, he can't help but feel a spasm of jealousy and concern as he watches her being drawn into this new circle.

The influence of peer pressure becomes increasingly apparent as Meher's interests and priorities seem to shift. She begins talking more about parties and social events that Prateek isn't invited to, her excitement noticeable as she recounts stories of these gatherings. Prateek, who has always been more introverted and focused on his studies, finds himself feeling out of step with this new version of Meher. He wants to be supportive but can't shake the feeling that he's being left behind. Adding to the complexity of their situation are the whispers and glances from their classmates.

High school is a breeding ground for gossip, and Prateek and Meher's relationship has not gone unnoticed. Prateek overhears bits of conversation in the hallways, talking about whether they're still together, whether Meher has moved on to someone else. These rumors, whether based in truth or not, plant seeds of doubt in Prateek's mind, fueling his growing insecurity. The pressure to conform to societal expectations of what a high school relationship should look like also begins to weigh on both Prateek and Meher. They see other couples around them engaging in public displays of affection, attending every school event together, and constantly posting about their relationship on social media. Prateek and Meher's more private, understated connection suddenly feels inadequate in comparison. Prateek finds himself wondering if Meher is disappointed that their relationship doesn't match up to these external ideals.

As these external pressures mount, Prateek notices a change in Meher's attitude towards their future plans. Where once they had eagerly discussed their dreams of attending the same college, now Meher seems hesitant to commit to any long term plans. When Prateek brings up the topic, she responds with hazy statements about keeping their options open and not wanting to limit themselves. This shift leaves Prateek feeling unsettled, wondering if Meher's changing perspective on their future together is a reflection of her changing feelings in the present. The strain of these changes begins to manifest in small arguments and misunderstandings. Topics that once would have been easily resolved now become points of contention. Prateek finds himself becoming more sensitive to perceived slights, while Meher seems increasingly irritated by his attempts to understand her behavior. Their once easy empathy is replaced by an undercurrent of tension that neither seems able to address directly.

In one particularly affecting moment, Prateek attempts to surprise Meher by showing up at her debate club meeting with her favorite snacks. He waits outside the classroom, excited to see her reaction. When Meher emerges, surrounded by her new friends, she seems more embarrassed than pleased by his gesture. She quickly thanks him, takes the snacks, and hurries off with her group, leaving Prateek standing alone in the hallway, feeling foolish and out of place. This incident serves as a catalyst for Prateek to confront the reality of their changing relationship. He realizes that the cracks in their connection are no longer something he can ignore or explain away. The fantasy of their perfect love story is crumbling, replaced by the harsh light of reality and the complexities of growing up. As Prateek grapples with these realizations, he finds himself torn between his deep feelings for Meher and his growing awareness that something fundamental has shifted between them. He wants to fight for their relationship, to recapture the magic of their early days together. But he also begins to question whether his efforts are useless, whether Meher's heart has already moved on while he wasn't looking.

The internal struggle Prateek faces is intense. On one hand, his love for Meher remains strong, and the thought of losing her is almost unbearable. He recalls all the beautiful moments they've shared, the ways in which she's enriched his life, and he can't imagine a future without her by his side. On the other hand, he's forced to confront the possibility that holding on too tightly might only push Meher further away.

As this chapter draws to a close, Prateek finds himself at a crossroads. The once clear path of his relationship with Meher has become tangled and uncertain. He knows that he needs to address these changes head-on, to have an honest conversation with Meher about where they stand. But fear holds him back—fear of what he might learn, fear of losing the girl he loves, fear of having to face a future different from the one he had imagined. The cracks in their relationship's foundation have become impossible to ignore, setting the stage for the difficult conversations and decisions that lie ahead. As we move into the next chapter, the question looms: Will Prateek find the courage to confront these issues with Meher, and how will she respond when he does? The turning point in their relationship is approaching, promising to test the strength of their bond and the depth of their feelings for each other.

CHAPTER SIX

THE CHANGES IN WIND

The winds of change have begun to blow, carrying with them the seeds of uncertainty and potential heartbreak. The turning point in their relationship became increasingly apparent as Meher's interest began to change. What was once a vibrant connection, filled with shared laughter and stolen glances, now felt muted and distant. Prateek, still deeply in love, found himself grappling with a new reality that he struggled to comprehend. The school van, once their sanctuary of budding romance, now felt like a confined space of awkward silences and unspoken tensions.

Meher's behavior shifted subtly at first, but as days turned into weeks, the changes became impossible for Prateek to ignore. Her bright smiles, once reserved for him, seemed to dim in his presence. The playful jokes that had characterized their interactions gave way to short, hasty responses. Prateek found himself reaching for conversations, trying to recapture the bond they once shared, only to be met with Meher's apparent disinterest. In moments of solitude, Prateek replayed their recent interactions, searching for clues that might explain the sudden change. Had he said something wrong? Was there an unseen offense that had caused this break? The more he thought, the more confused he became. The girl who had once seemed to hang on his every word now appeared distant and preoccupied, her mind clearly elsewhere during their time together. Prateek's emotional turbulence manifested in various ways. Some days, he would attempt to bridge the growing gap with grand gestures – bringing Meher her favorite snacks or offering to help with her homework. Other days, he retreated into himself, hoping that giving her space might rekindle her interest. The constant oscillation between action and inaction left him exhausted and increasingly anxious.

As the emotional distance between them grew, Prateek found himself desperate to communicate with Meher about the shift in their relationship. He crafted careful messages, poring over each word, hoping to strike the right balance between concern and casual inquiry. "Hey, is everything okay? You seem a bit distant lately," he would type, only to delete and rephrase countless times before finally hitting send. Meher's responses to these attempts at communication were frustratingly vague. "Everything's fine," she would reply, or "Just busy with school stuff." These brief messages only served to deepen Prateek's confusion and hurt. He longed for the open, honest conversations they once shared, where no topic was off-limits, and laughter came easily.

The school van, once a haven for their blossoming romance, became a daily exercise in emotional restraint for Prateek. He found himself aware of Meher's every movement – the way she would look out the window instead of meeting his gaze, how she seemed to lean away from him rather than toward him as she once did. The physical presence only emphasized the emotional gap that had opened between them. In his attempts to understand the situation, Prateek began to notice changes in Meher's social interactions beyond their relationship. She seemed to be spending more time with a different group of friends, laughing and chatting in a way that painfully reminded him of how they used to be. This observation added a new layer of complexity to his emotional struggle – a tone of jealousy mixed with a growing fear that he was being left behind. Meher's unwillingness to share her feelings became increasingly visible as Prateek's attempts to reconnect were met with polite but firm deflections. "I'm just going through some stuff," she would say, her eyes avoiding his. "It's nothing you need to worry about." But for Prateek, these dismissals only fueled his worry and intensified his desire to understand and help.

As days turned into weeks, Prateek began to sense that Meher's internal struggles went beyond their relationship. He caught glimpses of a heaviness in her eyes, a weariness in her appearance that suggested she was grappling with issues she wasn't ready or willing to share. This realization brought with it a new kind of pain for Prateek – the ache of seeing someone he cared for deeply struggling and feeling powerless to help. The once-clear waters of their relationship had become dull, filled with unspoken words and hidden currents. Prateek found himself navigating this new terrain with fear, unsure of where he stood or how to proceed. Every interaction felt burdened with potential meaning, every word carefully weighed for fear of widening the gap between them. As Prateek struggled to make sense of the changing dynamics, he couldn't help but reflect on the nature of teenage love. He had entered this relationship with the boundless hope of youth, believing that the strength of his feelings could overcome any obstacle. Now, faced with the reality of Meher's disappearing interest, he was forced to confront the fragility of young romance and the complexities of human emotions.

The change in Meher wasn't just affecting their romantic relationship; it was reshaping the entire landscape of Prateek's social world. Friends who had become accustomed to seeing them as a unit now looked on with curiosity and concern. Prateek found himself fielding questions he couldn't answer, forcing a smile and assuring everyone that things were fine, even as doubt tortured him. In quiet moments, Prateek allowed himself to indulge in memories of happier times – the shy smiles exchanged across the classroom, the thrill of their first hand-hold, the warmth of Meher's laughter. These recollections, once a source of joy, now carried a bittersweet tone. They served as both a reminder of what he feared losing and a spark of hope that perhaps those feelings could be rekindled.

As the emotional distance between them grew, Prateek found himself struggling with a profound sense of loss. It wasn't just the potential end of a romantic relationship he was mourning, but the loss of a confidante, a partner in adventure, someone who had come to occupy a central role in his daily life. The blank left by Meher's emotional withdrawal seemed to diffuse every aspect of his existence. The turning point in their relationship wasn't marked by a single dramatic event, but rather a series of small moments that collectively signaled a shift. It was in the way Meher's hand no longer sought his during their van rides, how her gaze would drift past him rather than meeting his eyes, the increasing frequency with which she quoted homework or family obligations as reasons to cut their time together short. Each instance alone might have been dismissed, but together they painted a clear picture of change. Despite the pain of Meher's emotional withdrawal, Prateek found himself unable to let go of the hope that they might reconnect next year. He oscillated between giving her space and making hesitant approaches, each approach fraught with anxiety and the fear of further rejection. This constant state of emotional uncertainty left him feeling drained and increasingly desperate for resolution, one way or another.

As Meher's behavior continued to puzzle and hurt him, Prateek began to seek understanding from other sources. He confided in close friends, pored over relationship advice in magazines and online forums, and even considered seeking guidance from a school counselor. These efforts to make sense of his situation provided some comfort but ultimately underscored the uniquely personal nature of their relationship struggles. In his more self-analytical moments, Prateek began to recognize that the pain he was experiencing was part of a larger process of growth and self-discovery. He realized that navigating this difficult period was teaching him valuable lessons about resilience, emotional intelligence, and the complex nature of human relationships. While this understanding didn't diminish his immediate hurt, it provided a glimmer of hope for personal growth amidst the turbulence.

As the chapter draws to a close, we find Prateek standing at a crossroads, caught between his enduring feelings for Meher and the growing realization that their relationship has fundamentally changed. The once-clear path of their romance has become overgrown with doubts, unspoken words, and shifting emotions. As we move forward, the question remains: will Prateek find a way to bridge the growing gap between them, or will he be forced to accept that sometimes, love alone is not enough to keep two people together? This pivotal moment in Prateek and Meher's story sets the stage for the emotional confrontation that lies ahead.

As we transition into the next chapter, we will see how Prateek's determination to understand and potentially salvage their relationship collides with Meher's own journey of self discovery and changing priorities. The stage is set for a candid and potentially heart-wrenching dialogue that will shape the course of their future interactions and test the strength of their bond.

CHAPTER SEVEN

HOLDING ON

As we transition from the thundering events of the previous chapter, we find Prateek at a crossroads, grappling with the sudden shift in his relationship with Meher. The once-vibrant connection between them has begun to fade, leaving Prateek in a state of emotional turmoil. Yet, despite the growing distance, he remains steadfast in his determination to save what they once had. Prateek's resolve to win Meher back was not born out of mere stubbornness or a refusal to accept reality. It stemmed from a deep-seated belief in the authenticity of their connection, a bond that had blossomed in the confined space of their school van and flourished into something he believed was truly special.

As he sat in his room, surrounded by memories of their time together, Prateek couldn't help but feel a surge of determination crossing through his veins. He began to formulate plans, each more elaborate than the last, to reignite the spark that had seemingly dimmed in Meher's eyes. Perhaps, he thought, if he could recreate some of their most cherished moments, she would remember the magic they once shared. With this in mind, Prateek set a plan to invite her to the cafe where they first met, hoping that the familiar setting would stir something within Meher's heart. As he carefully prepared for this grand gesture, Prateek found himself constantly distracted by memories of happier times. These flashbacks served as both a source of comfort and a painful reminder of what he stood to lose. He recalled the way Meher's eyes would light up when he told one of his lame jokes, the sound of her laughter echoing through the van on their rides home. He remembered the gentle brush of her hand against his as they walked through the school corridors, a subtle yet electrifying gesture that never failed to send his heart racing. These bittersweet recollections only served to fuel Prateek's determination. He refused to believe that what they had shared could simply fade away. Surely, he thought, if he could just remind Meher of these moments, she would see that their connection was worth fighting for. He started leaving small gifts in Meher's desk and enlisted the help of their mutual friends to plan "chance" encounters. Each attempt was met with varying degrees of success, but none seemed to fully bridge the growing gap between them.

As Prateek's efforts intensified, so did the emotional toll on his soul. He found himself lying awake at night, replaying every interaction with Meher, analyzing her words and actions for any sign that she might be coming around. The constant state of uncertainty began to wear on him, affecting his schoolwork and his other relationships. His parents, noticing the change in their usually upbeat son, attempted to offer words of comfort and advice. **"First love is always the hardest,"** his mother had said gently one evening, finding Prateek brooding in the kitchen. "But remember, it's not the end of the world if things don't work out. You're young, and there's so much more life ahead of you." While Prateek appreciated their concern, he couldn't help but feel that they didn't truly understand. To him, Meher wasn't just a first love or a fleeting teenage romance. She was the person who had awakened something within him, who had shown him a depth of feeling he hadn't known he was capable of experiencing. The thought of losing her felt like losing a part of himself.

As the days turned into weeks, Prateek's friends began to express concern over his single-minded focus on winning Meher back. His friend, Sohum, attempted to intervene during a particularly low moment. "I know you care about her, man," Sohum said, his voice filled with genuine concern, "but you can't keep putting your life on hold like this. Maybe it's time to accept that things have changed and try to move on." Prateek bristled at the suggestion, unable to understand the idea of giving up on what he believed was the most significant relationship of his life. "You don't understand," he replied, his voice tight with emotion. "What Meher and I have... it's special. I can't just walk away from that." Yet, even as he defended his actions to his friends, a small part of Prateek couldn't help but wonder if they might be right.

Was he holding on to something that was already slipping away? The doubt attacked him, creating a constant internal conflict between his heart's desire and the harsh realities he was facing. In an attempt to gain some perspective, Prateek found himself revisiting the places that held special significance in his relationship with Meher. He wandered through the school hallways where they had spent countless hours bunking the classes, and even drove past the ice cream parlor where they had shared their first ice cream date.

In the days that followed, Prateek found himself at a crossroads. He was torn between his unwavering love for Meher and the growing realization that perhaps, despite his best efforts, he couldn't force her to feel the same way. The internal struggle manifested in sleepless nights and distracted days, as he grappled with the possibility that sometimes, love alone isn't enough to keep two people together. It was during one of these restless nights that Prateek stumbled upon a quote that resonated deeply with him. Scribbled in the margin of an old notebook, the words of Kahlil Gibran stared back at him: **"If you love someone let them go, for if they return, they were always yours. If they don't, they never were."** The simplicity and profundity of these words struck a chord within him, prompting a moment of self-observation.

For the first time since Meher had begun to pull away, Prateek allowed himself to consider the possibility of letting go. Not out of resignation or defeat, but out of a deep and abiding love that prioritized her happiness over his own desires. It was a painful realization, one that brought with it a flood of emotions – grief, fear, and a strange sense of liberation.

As dawn broke, casting a soft light through his bedroom window, Prateek made a decision. He would make one last, heartfelt attempt to connect with Meher, to open up his feelings and hopes for their relationship. But if she still chose to walk away, he would respect her decision, no matter how much it hurt. With this newfound resolve, Prateek began to craft a letter to Meher, pouring his heart onto the page. He wrote of their shared memories, of the love he still held for her, and of his hopes for their future – whether together or apart. As he wrote, he felt a weight lifting from his shoulders, replaced by a bittersweet acceptance of whatever the future might hold.

As we leave Prateek at this pivotal moment, penning his heartfelt feelings to Meher, we can't help but wonder about the outcome. Will his words reach her heart, rekindling the flame that once burned so brightly between them? Or will this letter serve as a final chapter in their shared story? As we move forward, we'll see how this act of vulnerability and honesty shapes the course of their relationship, and how it affects Prateek's journey of self-discovery and growth.

THE HEARTBREAK

Building on the emotional journey established in the previous chapters, we now dive into the heart-wrenching reality of Prateek's silent heartbreak. The once vibrant connection between Prateek and Meher has collapsed, leaving Prateek to grapple with a profound sense of isolation and despair.

As the days stretched into weeks, Prateek found himself increasingly alone in the very spaces that once held so much joy. The school van, once a sanctuary of shared laughter and stolen glances, now felt suffocating. Meher's presence, though physically near, seemed distant and unreachable. Prateek would steal glances at her, hoping to catch her eye, to see a flicker of the warmth that used to be there. But more often than not, he was met with prevented gazes, impersonal smiles that cut deeper than any harsh word could. The silence between them was deafening. Where once their conversations flowed effortlessly, now every attempt at communication felt forced and awkward.

Prateek replayed their past interactions in his mind, desperately trying to pinpoint where things had gone wrong. Was it something he said? Something he did? The uncertainty tortured him, leaving him feeling hollow and lost.

This emotional turmoil began to take its toll on Prateek's daily life. His grades, once a source of pride, started to slip. Teachers who had known him as an engaged and enthusiastic student now saw a distracted, withdrawn young man. Kiara, his best female friend, pulled him aside after class one day, her eyes filled with concern. "Prateek, is everything alright? You seem... different lately." Prateek managed a weak smile and mumbled something about being tired, but the truth was screaming inside him. How could he explain that his world was crumbling, all because of a love he couldn't let go of?

Nights became a battlefield of restless thoughts and dreams haunted by Meher's smile. Prateek would toss and turn, his mind racing with scenarios of what he could say or do to bridge the growing distance between them. But each morning, as he saw Meher in the school hallways, surrounded by her friends and seemingly carefree, his resolve would crumble. The Meher he knew, the one who had shared her dreams and fears with him in hushed whispers, seemed to have vanished, replaced by a stranger who wore her face but didn't see him at all. The cafeteria, once a place of shared lunches and playful banter, became a daily exercise in heartache. Prateek would watch as Meher sat with her group of friends, her laughter floating across the room like a bittersweet melody. He longed to be the one making her laugh, to see her eyes light up the way they used to when she looked at him. Instead, he found himself sitting alone more often than not, pushing food around his tiffin and trying to ignore the pitying glances from classmates who had noticed the change. Prateek's attempts at casual conversation became strained, laced with questions about her social life. He found himself making excuses to be in the same places as her, hoping for a chance encounter that might rekindle their connection. But each time, he was met with polite disinterest or, worse, genuine confusion at his behavior.

As the weeks wore on, Prateek's emotional state began to take a visible toll on his appearance. Dark circles appeared under his eyes from nights spent tossing and turning. His usually neat appearance became messy, and his clothes wrinkled. He caught sight of himself in the mirror one morning and barely recognized the person staring back at him. This wasn't the Prateek that Meher had fallen for, the confident and caring boy with dreams and ambitions. This was a shadow, a shell of his former self. It was during a particularly low moment, sitting alone in his room surrounded by memories of his time with Meher, that Prateek had a moment of clarity. He picked up a photo of them together, taken during happier times. Their smiles were radiant, their eyes locked on each other as if nothing else in the world mattered. Prateek traced Meher's face with his finger, remembering the feel of her skin, the sound of her laugh. And in that moment, he realized that by holding on so tightly to what was, he was losing sight of who he was. This realization didn't magically erase the pain or make hisfeelings for Meher disappear. But it did plant a seed of change in Prateek's mind. He began to understand that his worth wasn't defined by Meher's affection, that there was more to him than just being her boyfriend. It was a small step, but an important one on the path to healing.

The next day at school, Prateek made a conscious effort to engage with his friends again. He joined them for lunch, forcing himself to participate in their conversations even when his heart wasn't in it. It felt strange at first, almost like he was betraying his feelings for Meher by trying to move on. But as the day progressed, he found moments of genuine laughter and friendship that he had been missing for weeks. Meher noticed the change in Prateek, subtle though it was.

As they passed each other in the hallway, their eyes met for a brief moment. There was a flicker of something in her gaze — surprise, perhaps, or a hint of the warmth that used to be there. Prateek felt his heart race, hope surging through him. But he forced himself to keep walking, to not read too much into a fleeting glance.

The pain of Meher's distance is still there, a constant ache in his chest. But there's also a glimmer of something else — a realization that life goes on, that he is more than just his heartbreak. It's a fragile balance, teetering between the pull of the past and the possibility of the future. The journey ahead is uncertain, filled with the potential for more hurt but also the promise of growth and healing. As Prateek lies in bed that night, staring at the ceiling, he allows himself to imagine a future where the pain isn't so raw, where Meher's memory doesn't consume his every waking thought.

It's a small step, but an important one.

This chapter serves as a turning point in Prateek's emotional journey, setting the stage for the confrontation and decisions that lie ahead. The silent heartbreak he has endured has changed him, forcing him to confront not just his feelings for Meher, but his own identity and sense of self-worth. As we move forward, the question remains: will Prateek find the strength to truly move on, or will his love for Meher continue to define his path?

CHAPTER NINE

CONFRONTATION

Building upon the emotional journey of Prateek and Meher established in the previous chapters, we now arrive at a critical juncture in their relationship. The silent heartbreak that Prateek endured in Chapter 8 has reached its boiling point, leading to an inevitable confrontation that will shape the course of their future interactions.

As the school van rumbled along its familiar route, the air inside was thick with tension. Prateek sat rigidly in his seat, his eyes fixed on Meher, who seemed determined to look anywhere but at him. The once-comfortable silence between them had turned into an oppressive weight, pushing down on Prateek's chest until he felt he could barely breathe. He knew that this moment, this ride, would be the catalyst for the conversation they had both been avoiding. When the van finally stopped, and the other students filed out, Prateek reached out and gently touched Meher's arm. **"Can we talk?"** he asked, his voice barely above a whisper. Meher hesitated for a moment, her eyes flickering with an emotion Prateek couldn't quite interpret, before she nodded slowly. They found a quiet spot beneath an old oak tree on the school grounds, its branches providing a canopy of privacy. Prateek's heart raced as he struggled to find the right words to begin. He had rehearsed this conversation countless times in his mind, but now, face-to-face with Meher, all his carefully prepared speeches seemed to evaporate. **"What's happening to us, Meher?"** Prateek finally blurted out, his voice cracking with emotion. **"I feel like I'm losing you, and I don't even know why."** Meher's gaze dropped to the ground, her fingers absently plucking at blades of grass. **"I don't know,** Prateek," she replied softly. **"Things are just... different now."** Prateek felt a surge of frustration at her unclear response. "Different how? What changed? Was it something I did? Something I said?" The questions tumbled out of him, each one laced with the fear and confusion that had been building for weeks. Meher looked up at him then, her eyes shimmering with unshed tears. **"It's not you, Prateek. It's me. I'm changing, and I don't know how to explain it."** The platitude of her words stung Prateek, and he couldn't help but let out a bitter laugh. "That's what people say when they don't want to hurt someone's feelings. But I'm already hurt, Meher. I'm hurting every day, watching you pull away from me."

His raw honesty seemed to break something open in Meher. She took a deep breath, as if steeling herself for what she was about to say. **"I'm scared, Prateek. I'm scared of long term commitments. It's overwhelming, and I don't know if I'm ready for it and I don't have the same feelings as they were before."**

Prateek felt a glimmer of hope at her admission. She lost her feelings for him; it wasn't all in his head. "But that's okay, isn't it?" he asked eagerly. "We can figure it out together. We don't have to rush anything."

The words hung in the air between them, heavy with implication.

Prateek's mind raced, trying to find a solution, a way to keep Meher close while giving her the space she needed. "We can do that," he insisted. "We can give each other space. I can back off, let you have time for your other interests."

But even as he said it, he could see the doubt in Meher's eyes. She reached out and took his hand, her touch sending familiar sparks through his body.

"Prateek, you're one of the most important people in my life. But I think... I think I need more than just space."

The finality in her tone made Prateek's heart ache, "Are you breaking up with me?" he asked, his voice barely audible.

Meher's silence was answer enough.

Prateek felt tears welling up in his eyes, and he didn't bother to hide them. "I love you, Meher," he said, his voice breaking. "I've never felt this way about anyone before. How can you just throw that away?"

Meher's own tears spilled over then. "I'm not throwing it away, Prateek. I'm trying to do what's right for both of us. We're so young, and there's so much ahead of us. I don't want to look back years from now and regret not taking the time to figure out who we are as individuals."

Prateek wanted to argue, to tell her that he already knew who he was and that she was a part of that. But a small, rational part of his brain understood what she was saying. They were young, and the intensity of his feelings was both exhilarating and terrifying.

"So that's it?" he asked, unable to keep the bitterness from his voice. "We just go back to being friends?"

Meher squeezed his hand. "I hope we can. You mean too much to me to lose you completely, Prateek."

The idea of being just friends with Meher felt like a knife twisting in Prateek's heart.

How could he go back to that when he knew what it was like to hold her, to kiss her, to be loved by her? But the alternative – losing her entirely – was even more unbearable.

"I don't know if I can do that," Prateek admitted, his voice thick with emotion. "I don't know how to stop loving you."

Meher's face crumpled at his words. "I'm not asking you to stop loving me, Prateek. I'm just asking for time and space to grow. Maybe... maybe someday..."

She left the sentence unfinished, and Prateek felt a flicker of hope ignite in his chest. Maybe someday, when they were older and more sure of themselves, they could find their way back to each other.

As they sat there under the oak tree, the weight of their conversation settling around them, Prateek realized that this was a turning point not just in their relationship, but in their lives. They were navigating the complexities of love and identity, trying to balance their feelings for each other with their need for individual growth. The bell rang in the distance, signaling the start of classes.

Meher stood up "We should go," she said softly. Prateek nodded, slowly getting to his feet. As they walked back towards the school building, he felt a strange mix of emotions – heartbreak, confusion, a glimmer of hope, and an overwhelming sense of loss. He knew that things would be different now, that the easy comfort they once shared would be replaced by awkward silences and stolen glances. But as they reached the school doors, Meher turned to him one last time. "Thank you for understanding, Prateek," she said, her voice barely above a whisper. "And for loving me."

With those words, she disappeared into the crowded hallway, leaving Prateek standing alone, his heart in pieces but with a newfound understanding of the complexities of love and growth. As he slowly made his way to his first class, he couldn't help but wonder what the future held for them, and how this moment would shape the decisions that lay ahead in the coming chapters of their lives.

The emotional confrontation between Prateek and Meher marked a significant shift in their relationship, setting the stage for the difficult decisions and personal growth that would follow. As Prateek grappled with the aftermath of their conversation, he would soon find himself facing a crossroads, forced to confront the reality of their changing dynamic and the possibility of a future without Meher by his side. The school day passed in a blur for Prateek, his mind replaying every word, every expression from his conversation with Meher. He found himself unable to focus on his classes, instead staring out the window, lost in thought. The finality of Meher's words echoed in his mind, each repetition feeling like a fresh wound to his heart. As the final bell rang, Prateek made his way to the school van, his feet heavy with dread. He knew that the ride home would be different now, that the seat next to Meher, once a place of comfort and joy, would now feel like a reminder of what he had lost.

When he boarded the van, he saw Meher already seated, her gaze fixed on a book in her lap. For a moment, Prateek hesitated, unsure whether to take his usual seat beside her or find another spot. In the end, habit won out, and he slid into the familiar seat, acutely aware of the invisible barrier that now existed between them. The van journey, once filled with laughter and shared secrets, was now painfully silent. Prateek could feel the eyes of their fellow students on them, curious about the sudden change in dynamics between the couple who had been inseparable for months.

As they neared Meher's stop, Prateek felt a sudden panic. This was usually when they would make plans to meet up later or share a quick goodbye. Now, he didn't know what to do or say. Meher solved the dilemma for him, offering a small, sad smile as she gathered her things. Prateek waved his hand for goodbye, unable to form words around the lump in his throat. He watched as Meher made her way down the van aisle, her figure disappearing into the afternoon sunlight. It felt symbolic somehow, as if she was walking out not just of the van but of his life. The rest of the ride home was a blur of conflicting emotions for Prateek. Part of him wanted to run after Meher, to beg her to reconsider, to promise her that he could be whatever she needed him to be. Another part recognized the truth in her words, understanding that at teenage, they were both still discovering who they were as individuals.

As he lay in bed that night, staring at the ceiling, Prateek's mind raced with questions and doubts. Had he done something wrong? Could he have been a better boyfriend? Was there still a chance for them, or had Meher already moved on in her heart?

He reached for his phone, his fingers hovering over Meher's name in his contacts. How many times had he called her at this hour, just to hear her voice before he fell asleep?

Now, the thought of hearing her voicemail message was almost too painful to bear.Instead, Prateek found himself scrolling through their old text messages, reliving the happier moments of their relationship. Each declaration of love, each inside joke, each heart emoji felt like a knife twisting in his chest. He wondered if Meher was doing the same thing, if she was lying awake missing him as much as he missed her. As the night wore on, Prateek's thoughts turned to the future. What would school be like now? How would he face seeing Meher every day, knowing that they were no longer together?

The thought of watching her move on, possibly with someone else, filled him with a mixture of dread and jealousy. But amidst the pain and confusion, a small voice in the back of Prateek's mind whispered that maybe, just maybe, Meher was right. Maybe they did need time to grow as individuals. Maybe this wasn't the end of their story, but merely a chapter in a longer narrative.

With that thought, Prateek finally drifted off to sleep, his dreams filled with memories of Meher's smile and the hope that someday, they might find their way back to each other. The days that followed were a test of Prateek's emotional strength. Each morning, he would steel himself for the van ride, preparing for the awkward silences and stolen glances that had replaced their once easy companionship. He found himself hyper-aware of Meher's every movement, analyzing each smile or frown, desperately seeking any sign that she might be reconsidering her decision.

In class, Prateek struggled to concentrate, his mind constantly wandering to thoughts of Meher. He caught himself doodling her name in the margins of his notebook, only to hastily scribble it out when he realized what he was doing. His grades began to slip, a fact that didn't go unnoticed by his teachers or his parents.

Lunch periods, once a highlight of Prateek's day when he could sit with Meher and their friends, became an exercise in avoidance. He found himself making excuses to eat alone in the empty classrooms, unable to bear the sight of Meher laughing and chatting with others as if their breakup hadn't affected her at all. But even as Prateek grappled with his heartache, he couldn't help but notice subtle changes in Meher. There were moments when he caught her looking at him with an expression of longing, quickly masked when she realized he had seen. Sometimes, in the van, he would feel her shift slightly closer to him, as if drawn by an invisible force, only to pull away again. These small moments gave Prateek hope, fueling his determination to win Meher back. He began to plan grand gestures, thinking of ways to show her that they belonged together. He considered writing her love letters, chanting her name outside her window, or orchestrating elaborate surprises to remind her of their happiest times together. Yet each time he was on the urge of acting on these impulses, Prateek would remember Meher's words about needing space to grow. He realized that pushing too hard might only drive her further away. So, he held back, his heart aching with every restrained action and unspoken word.

As weeks passed, Prateek found himself caught in a cycle of hope and despair. Some days, he felt sure that Meher would come back to him, that their love was too strong to be denied. Other days, the sight of her talking animatedly with other boys in their class would send him spiraling into jealousy and self-doubt. Through it all, Prateek clung to the memories of their time together. He replayed their first meet in his mind, remembering the softness of Meher's hands and the way his heart had raced. He thought about the lazy Sunday afternoons they had spent together, talking about their dreams for the future. Each memory was both a comfort and a torture, reminding him of what he had lost.

One particularly difficult day, Prateek found himself back under the old oak tree where they had their confrontation. As he sat there, lost in thought, he was startled by a familiar voice. "I thought I might find you here," Meher said softly, lowering herself to sit beside him.

Prateek's heart melted at her presence, even as he tried to maintain a calm exterior. "Just needed some air," he replied, his voice tangled with emotion.

Meher nodded, her eyes scanning the familiar landscape of the school grounds. "I miss you, Prateek," she admitted after a long silence. "I miss us."

Her words sent a knock through Prateek's body. He turned to look at her, searching her face for any sign of what she might be thinking.

"I miss you too," he said simply, afraid to say more and break the fragile moment.

Meher sighed, leaning back against the tree trunk. "But I still think we made the right decision," she continued, her voice tinged with sadness. "These past few weeks... they've been hard, but I've learned so much about myself."

Prateek felt a mixture of hope and disappointment wash over him.

"And what have you learned?" he asked, trying to keep the desperation out of his voice.

Meher was quiet for a moment, gathering her thoughts. "I've learned that I'm stronger than I thought," she said finally. "That I can stand on my own. But I've also learned how much you mean to me, Prateek. How much our friendship means to me."

The word 'friendship' stung, but Prateek forced himself to focus on the positive aspects of what Meher was saying.

"So where does that leave us?" he asked, his voice barely above a whisper.

Meher turned to look at him, her eyes filled with a mixture of affection and uncertainty. "I don't know," she admitted. "But I do know that I don't want to lose you from my life, Prateek.

Can we... can we try to be friends? Real friends, not just exes who avoid each other?"

Prateek felt his heart constrict at her words. The idea of being 'just friends' with Meher was painful, but the alternative – not having her in his life at all – was unthinkable.

He took a deep breath, weighing his response carefully.

"I'd like that," he said finally, managing a small smile. "It won't be easy, but I want you in my life too, Meher. In whatever way I can have you."

Meher's face lit up with relief, and she impulsively reached out to squeeze his hand.

The familiar touch sent sparks through Prateek's body, reminding him of all they had shared and all he had lost. But there was also a comfort in the gesture, a promise of a connection that, while changed, was not entirely broken.

As they sat there under the oak tree, a gentle breeze rustling the leaves above them, Prateek felt a shift in the air between them. The tension that had been present since their breakup seemed to ease slightly, replaced by a tentative understanding. They were entering new territory, navigating the complexities of a relationship that was no longer romantic but still deeply meaningful.

Prateek knew that the path ahead would not be easy. His feelings for Meher were still strong, and learning to see her as just a friend would be a daily challenge. There would be moments of jealousy, of longing, of wishing for what once was. But as he looked at Meher, saw the mix of emotions playing across her face, he realized that this new chapter in their relationship could be valuable in its own way. As the sun began to set, casting long shadows across the school grounds, Prateek and Meher stood up, brushing grass from their clothes. They walked back towards the parking lot in companionable silence, each lost in their own thoughts about the future.

Before they parted ways, Meher turned to Prateek one last time. "Thank you," she said softly. "For understanding, for being you."

Prateek nodded, his throat tight with emotion. "Always," he managed to say.

As he watched Meher walk away, Prateek felt a strange mix of sadness and hope.

Their conversation had not magically fixed everything, but it had opened a door to a new kind of relationship. And who knew what the future might hold?

With a deep breath, Prateek turned and began the walk home, his mind already racing with thoughts of what this new friendship with Meher might look like. As he walked, he couldn't help but feel that this was not the end of their story, but perhaps the beginning of a new chapter, one filled with growth, understanding, and the possibility of a love that could evolve and mature alongside them. The emotional rollercoaster that Prateek had been riding since his confrontation with Meher began to settle into a new rhythm. The acute pain of their breakup gradually dulled to a persistent ache, ever-present but manageable.

As days turned into weeks, Prateek found himself adapting to this new reality, learning to navigate the complex terrain of being friends with someone he still had deep feelings for. Their interactions in the school van, once a source of tension and awkwardness, slowly began to regain some of their former ease. Prateek and Meher started to talk again, tentatively at first, about safe topics like schoolwork and mutual friends.

Gradually, their conversations deepened, touching on their individual experiences and personal growth since the breakup. Prateek found himself genuinely interested in Meher's new pursuits. She had joined the school's debate team and was excelling, her natural charm and quick wit making her a formidable opponent. While part of him felt a twinge of jealousy at the time she was spending with her new teammates, he couldn't help but feel proud of her accomplishments. For her part, Meher showed a sincere interest in Prateek's life as well. She encouraged him when he decided to try out for the school play, something he had always wanted to do but had never found the courage for before. When he landed a supporting role, Meher was one of the first to congratulate him, her genuine happiness for him warming his heart. These positive interactions, however, were interspersed with moments of heartache for Prateek. Seeing Meher laugh with other boys in the hallways or hearing about her weekend plans that didn't include him still stung.

There were nights when he lay awake, replaying their happiest moments together and wondering if he would ever feel that way again. As the school year progressed, Prateek and Meher's friendship continued to evolve. They found a comfortable rhythm, able to share parts of their lives with each other without the intense emotions that had characterized their romantic relationship. They studied together for exams, offered each other advice on personal matters, and even started to joke about their past relationship, finding humor in some of their more dramatic moments.

One afternoon, as they sat in their usual spot under the oak tree, Meher turned to Prateek with a thoughtful expression. "Do you ever wonder what would have happened if we had stayed together?" she asked softly.

Prateek felt a familiar pain in his chest, but it was duller now, more nostalgic than painful. "Sometimes," he admitted. "But I think... I think this is how it was supposed to be. We've both grown so much in the past few months."

Meher nodded, a small smile playing on her lips. "We have, haven't we? I'm proud of us, Prateek. For getting through this, for staying friends."

As they sat there, looking back about their shared experiences and discussing their hopes for the future, Prateek realized how far they had come. The raw pain of their breakup had transformed into a deeper understanding of themselves and each other.

Their love story hadn't ended; it had simply changed form, evolving into something equally valuable. His first love had not been the fairytale ending he had once imagined, but it had been real and meaningful. It had taught him about the complexities of emotions, the importance of personal growth, and the value of true friendship.

Walking home, Prateek reflected on the journey he and Meher had been through. From the first sparks of attraction to the heights of young love, through the pain of separation and the challenges of redefining their relationship, they had emerged stronger and wiser. Their story was not over; it was simply entering a new chapter, one filled with possibilities and the potential for continued growth and connection.

As Prateek reached his house, he paused to look back at the path he had walked, both literally and figuratively. The sun had almost set now, painting the sky in brilliant hues of orange and pink. It was a beautiful sight, reminding him that endings could also be beginnings, that change, while sometimes painful, could lead to unexpected beauty.

With a deep breath and a smile, Prateek turned and walked into his house, ready to embrace whatever the future might hold. His first love had shaped him, challenged him, and ultimately helped him grow. And as he closed the door behind him, he knew that whatever lay ahead, he would face it with the strength, wisdom, and open heart that his experiences with Meher had helped him develop.

The story of Prateek and Meher had not ended. It had simply transformed, becoming a part of the rich tapestry of experiences that would continue to shape their lives as they moved forward into the next stages of their journey.

Maybe in a parallel realm, they are together, their hearts align, where distance fades and love will shine, where time and distance dare not sever...